W9-AHA-820

Reagandoodle & Little Buddy
Find a Forever Family

Sandi Swiridoff with Wendy Dunham

Illustrated by Michal Sparks

HARVEST HOUSE PUBLISHERS
EUGENE, OREGON

Cover design by Mary Eakin Design

Interior design by Left Coast Design

Published in association with William K. Jensen Literary Agency, 119 Bampton Court, Eugene, Oregon 97404.

HARVEST KIDS is a trademark of The Hawkins Children's LLC. Harvest House Publishers, Inc., is the exclusive licensee of the trademark HARVEST KIDS.

Reagandoodle and Little Buddy Find a Forever Family
Copyright © 2019 by Sandi Swiridoff and Wendy Dunham
Illustrations © 2019 by Michal Sparks
Published by Harvest House Publishers
Eugene, Oregon 97408
www.harvesthousepublishers.com

ISBN 978-0-7369-7468-4 (hardcover)

Library of Congress Cataloging-in-Publication Data
 Names: Swiridoff, Sandi, author. | Dunham, Wendy, author. | Sparks, Michal, illustrator.
Title: Reagandoodle and Little Buddy find a forever family / Sandi Swiridoff with Wendy Dunham ; illustrations by
    Michal Sparks.
Description: Eugene, Oregon : Harvest House Publishers, [2019] | Summary:
   Reagan the Labradoodle tells Little Buddy all the wonderful things he has learned about being adopted. Includes
   note for children about God's plan. Identifiers: LCCN 2018061516 (print) | LCCN 2019000555 (ebook) | ISBN
   9780736974691 (ebook) | ISBN 9780736974684 (hardcover)
Subjects: | CYAC: Adoption—Fiction. | Dog adoption—Fiction. | Labradoodle—Fiction. | Dogs—Fiction. | Christian life—Fiction.
Classification: LCC PZ7.1.S948 (ebook) | LCC PZ7.1.S948 Re 2019 (print) | DDC [E]—dc23
LC record available at https://lccn.loc.gov/2018061516.

Printed in China

19 20 21 22 23 24 25 26 27/ LP / 10 9 8 7 6 5 4 3 2 1

My name is Reagandoodle, but you can call me Reagan.

And this is Little Buddy, my best friend.

REAGAN

Little Buddy

Since I'm older (at least in dog years), I'll be sharing our story.

When Little Buddy told me he was being
adopted, my tail wagged super-fast.

I was adopted too,
so I know how wonderful
that is.

When Little Buddy asked me what "adopted" means, I knew just what to say.

It means you're someone special. Someone chose you.
You're wanted, you're loved, you're adored.

It means you're part of a family.
You're not alone anymore.
You belong.

Being adopted means hearing "I love you!"
and saying, "I love you too!"

It's holding hands wherever you go.

There's no need to worry about getting lost.
You've already been found.

Being adopted means sitting on laps
that are just the right size,

spending time reading just the right books.

It's parents who
love you much deeper
than oceans,

whose love reaches far beyond skies.
You are loved more than the universe.

Being adopted means being cared for
when you're happy or sad,

when you're well or you're sick.
Someone will always watch over you.

When you're adopted,
cuddles and kisses will
never run out.

They will always be given to you.

Being adopted means birthday parties with candles and wishes. You are every reason to celebrate.

It's having a bed with soft downy pillows.
You will always have a place to rest your sleepy head.

It's sharing an afternoon snuggle-bug nap,
all arms crisscrossed and bear-hug wrapped.
You are safe and secure.

Being adopted means special times with Grandma
and Grandpa. You bring joy into their lives.

It's family
traditions.
Christmas tree
cutting, Easter
egg hunting,
family with family,
year after year.

You will always have memories to make.

Being adopted means being together. Eating, praying, loving, playing, everyone under one roof.

You make our house a home.

I looked at Little Buddy, who was smiling a very big smile, and I snuggled up against him.

"Little Buddy," I said, "adoption means all these things and even more. It means you have a forever family, just like me!"

Here are photos of the real Reagandoodle and Little Buddy. Reagandoodle is a special kind of dog called an Australian Labradoodle. When he was eight weeks old, he was adopted by Little Buddy's grandparents. Little Buddy became a

foster child when he was eleven months old. He was later adopted by his foster parents. Now he has a forever family just like Reagan.

Dear Precious Child,

Has anyone ever told you how incredibly important you are? You are so important that even before you were born, God knew everything about you. He knew whether you'd be a boy or a girl. He knew whether you'd run fast or slow. He knew whether you'd be adopted. He knew what your favorite ice cream would be. He even knew what family you would one day make complete.

Imagine that! The God of the whole world chose you to make a family complete! That means you are every reason your family is a family. Now *that's* important!

Always remember how loved and important you are to God, to your family, and to us!

With love, hugs, and plenty of doggie-licks,

Reagan and Little Buddy

*Pure and genuine religion in the sight of God
the Father means caring for the orphans.*
James 1:27

Do you have an adoption story you'd like to share? Little Buddy and I would love to hear it. You can email your story to us at Reagandoodle@ icloud.com.

Sandi Swiridoff is the "momager" of @Reagandoodle on Instagram. She and her husband, Eric, have two grown children and one famous fur-son (Reagan, of course). They are also very proud grandparents (one of their grandchildren being Little Buddy!). Besides spending time with her family, Sandi's greatest joy is using her gift of photography to bring smiles and encouragement to others while benefiting children in foster care. reagandoodle.com

Wendy Dunham is an award-winning inspirational children's and middle grade author, a registered therapist for children with special needs, and a blessed mama of two amazing grown-up kids. She is the author of two middle-grade novels: *My Name Is River* and its sequel, *Hope Girl*. She has a series of early readers titled Tales of Buttercup Grove. And in the Reagandoodle and Little Buddy series, Wendy writes as the voice of Reagandoodle. Please visit her website at wendydunhamauthor.com.

Michal Sparks' artwork can be found throughout the home-furnishings industry in textiles, gift items, dinnerware, and more. She is the artist for *Words of Comfort for Times of Loss, When Someone You Love Has Cancer,* and *A Simple Gift of Comfort,* as well as the Tales of Buttercup Grove series of children's books. Connect with Michal at www.michalsparks.com.